The
Tale
of
Jemima
Puddle-Duck

FREDERICK WARNE

Published by the Penguin Group
Penguin Books Ltd, 27 Wrights Lane, London W8 5TZ, England
Penguin Putnam Inc., 375 Hudson Street, New York, N.Y. 10014, USA
Penguin Books Canada Ltd, 10 Alcorn Avenue, Toronto, Ontario, Canada M4V 3B2
Penguin Books (NZ) Ltd, Private Bag 102902, NSMC, Auckland, New Zealand
Penguin Books India (P) Ltd, 11 Community Centre, Panchsheel Park, New Delhi 110 017, India
Penguin Books (South Africa) (Pty) Ltd, 5 Watkins Street, Denver Ext 4, 2094, South Africa

Penguin Books Ltd, Registered Offices: Harmondsworth, Middlesex, England

Visit our web site at: www.peterrabbit.com

This edition published by Frederick Warne 2001

1 3 5 7 9 10 8 6 4 2

ISBN: 07232 4719 6

Additional illustrations by Colin Twinn and Alex Vining

Colour reproduction by Saxon Photolitho
Printed and bound in Singapore by Tien Wah Press

The Tale of Jemima Puddle-Duck

Based on the original tale
BY BEATRIX POTTER

FREDERICK WARNE

This is the story of
Jemima Puddle-duck.

Jemima lived on a farm.
She wanted to hatch
her own eggs but the
farmer's wife would not
let her.

Jemima's sister, Rebeccah, did not want to hatch her own eggs.

"I would not look after them properly, and neither would you, Jemima," said Rebeccah.

Jemima tried to hide her eggs so that she could look after them.

But Jemima's eggs were always taken away from her.

One day Jemima left
the farm so she could lay
her eggs.

She wore a blue bonnet
and a pink shawl.

Jemima Puddle-duck ran down the hill and then jumped off into the air.

She flew over the tree-
tops looking for a place
to land.

Jemima landed in the wood and saw someone reading a newspaper.

"Quack?" said Jemima.

The gentleman looked
at Jemima. "Have you
lost your way?" he said.

Jemima told the
gentleman that she was
trying to find a place to
lay her eggs.

The gentleman said,
"I have a shed. You may
lay your eggs in there."

He opened the door and
let Jemima in.

The shed was full of feathers. It was very comfortable and soft. Jemima Puddle-duck made a nest.

She laid nine eggs.

The next day, the
gentleman said to
Jemima, "Let us have a
dinner party.

Bring some herbs from
the farm and I will make
an omelette."

Jemima met Kep.
He knew those herbs
were for cooking
roast duck!

Kep ran to the village
and told the puppies.

Jemima went back to
the wood and found
the gentleman.

He spoke in an angry voice. "Check your eggs and then come into my house. Quickly!"

Jemima felt afraid.

Kep and the puppies
found the shed in the
wood. They shut Jemima
in the shed to keep
her safe.

Then they chased the
gentleman away.
He never came back.

Kep opened the door of
the shed and let Jemima
Puddle-duck out.

Then Kep and the
puppies took Jemima
back to the farm.

Jemima laid some more
eggs and she was
allowed to hatch them
herself. She had four
yellow ducklings.